#

NO RULES FOR REX!

KEEP OFF
THE GRASS

by Daisy Alberto
illustrated by Jerry Smath

Kane Press, Inc.
New York

To Anthony Louis Bacigalupo IV—J. S.

Library of Congress Cataloging-in-Publication Data

Alberto, Daisy.
  No rules for Rex! / by Daisy Alberto ; illustrated by Jerry
Smath.
      p. cm. — (Social studies connects)
  "Civics - grades: K-2."
  Summary: Rex convinces his family to try a whole weekend without
rules.
  ISBN 1-57565-146-7 (pbk. : alk. paper)
  [1. Behavior—Fiction. 2. Rules (Philosophy)—Fiction. 3. Family
life—Fiction.] I. Smath, Jerry, ill. II. Title. III. Series.
  PZ7.A3217No 2005
  [E]—dc22
                            2004016958

10 9 8 7 6 5 4 3 2 1

First published in the United States of America in 2005 by Kane Press, Inc.
Printed in Hong Kong.

Social Studies Connects is a trademark of Kane Press, Inc.

Book Design: Edward Miller

www.kanepress.com

You would not believe the week I had. On
Monday, I brought my new Roboman to school.
Ms. Hayes snatched it up.

"That's against school rules, Rex!" she said.

Rules shmools, I thought.

Tuesday, after dinner, I played baseball. The bases were loaded. I was up at bat. Just then Rosie, my little sister, called, "Rex! Mom says to come in and do your homework!"

"We're in the middle of a game," I yelled back.

Rosie shrugged. "I don't make the rules."

I gave the bat to my friend, Steve, and stomped off.

On Wednesday night I started a library book.
I was just getting to the good part, when my dad
came in. "Lights out," he said.

"But Dad, the killer Cyclops is about to attack!"

"Sorry, kiddo. Bedtime," he said. "That's
the rule."

A **rule** tells people how they should
behave. Who makes the rules? Rules can
be made by a teacher, a family, even a
group of kids in a club. A rule that the
government makes is called a **law**.

On Thursday, we went on a class trip. Steve and I couldn't wait to ride the new roller coaster. But when we got to the front of the line, the ticket taker looked at me and shook his head.

"You're too short to ride, son," he said.

YOU MUST BE AS TALL AS THE DINO'S ARM TO RIDE THE ROLLER COASTER.

"That's not fair!" I complained. I pointed to Steve. "I'm just a tiny bit shorter than he is."

"Nope," he said. "The rule is, you have to be as tall as the dinosaur's arm."

What a bummer.

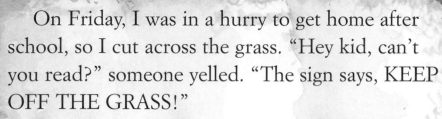

On Friday, I was in a hurry to get home after school, so I cut across the grass. "Hey kid, can't you read?" someone yelled. "The sign says, KEEP OFF THE GRASS!"

I looked around. There were rules everywhere!

ICE CREAM

PLEASE STAY IN LINE

BIKES ONLY

KEEP OFF THE GRASS

Signs help people remember rules and laws.

TRASH GOES HERE!

The police make sure people obey the laws. That's their job.

WYLIE PARK

RULES

Do not feed wildlife.
No campfires allowed.
Please be courteous!

STOP

KEEP DOGS ON LEASH

There were rules about where to walk and where to park. There were rules about where to throw your trash. There were even rules about how to walk your dog!

PLEASE DO NOT PICK THE FLOWERS

Now it's dinnertime. And just when I think that this week can't get any worse, I find out we're having *liver.*

Yuck! I hate liver! I make faces at Rosie while everyone else eats.

For dessert Mom brings out a fluffy lemon cream pie. Yum! I reach for a slice.

"Sorry, honey, no dessert until you've eaten your dinner," Mom says. "You know the rules."

"That's it!" I say. "Rules are ruining my life!" I'm so mad, I run outside.

Watch out!
There are consequences for breaking rules and laws. If you break a rule, you may not be allowed to have dessert or watch TV. People who break laws may have to pay fines—or even go to jail!

Everybody follows me. "Tell us what's bothering you," says Mom. So I do.

"You *have* had a tough week," Dad says.

"Sometimes," says Mom, "I get tired of rules."

"You do?" Rosie asks.

"Sure," Mom says. "Like when I can't use the express line at the market if I have more than 15 items—even if I have just 16 and I'm *really* in a rush!"

"I have an idea," I say. "How about we take a break from rules this weekend?"

Mom and Dad look at each other.

"Why not?" they say.

We all high five.

Then Mom brings me a giant slice of lemon pie. "Enjoy!" she says.

It's the best meal of my entire life.

Saturday morning I don't clean my room like I'm supposed to. This is the life!

I go downstairs. Rosie is watching her favorite movie, *Princess Patty and the Pink Pony*. Ugh. "When is this over?" I ask.

"Never." Rosie giggles. "I'm watching it again when it's done."

"You can't," I say. "We get to take turns picking shows."

"Why? Is that a rule?" Rosie asks sweetly.

"Ye . . . ," I start to say. Then I stop. I have to admit, the kid's pretty smart.

Steve and I spend the afternoon working on my new tree house. By the time we're done, I'm starving!

"So, what's for dinner?" I ask.

"Nothing," Mom says.

"What do you mean, nothing?" I say. "We have to have dinner! And Dad *always* cooks on Saturdays. That's the rule."

Mom shrugs. "Dad doesn't feel like cooking," she says. "You can make yourself a peanut butter and jelly sandwich."

"Make me one, too, while you're at it," calls Dad.

"Me too," says Mom.

"Me three," says Rosie.

I start to make the sandwiches. This isn't exactly how I imagined life without rules.

That night we play Monopoly. Rosie rolls the dice. "Six!" she says. She moves her piece six spaces and lands right on Go to Jail. "That roll doesn't count," she says. "I'm going to roll again."

Crime and punishment!
In early America, lawbreakers were often locked in wooden stocks in the town square. Sometimes people threw rotten fruit at them!

"Wait a minute," I say. "That's against the rules."

"What rules?" asks Rosie. Then she starts to laugh.

Oh no! I think I've created a monster!

Rules! Rules! Rules!
As a boy, George Washington copied down 110 rules for behavior. Here are a few: Do not stand when others are sitting. Do not laugh loudly in public. Do not spit in the fire. Do not leave your room unless you are fully dressed.

On Sunday, I have a soccer game. My room is such a disaster, it takes forever to find my cleats. When I do, they have sparkly purple flower stickers all over them. I'll be late for the game if I try to peel them off!

"Rosie!" I yell. "What did you do? You're not allowed in my room!"

Rosie peeks in. She looks like her feelings are hurt. "But there's no keep-out rule this weekend," she says. "And the stickers were a good-luck present for you. I'm sorry!"

"Sorry isn't good enough. You ruined my cleats!" I rush past Rosie and head toward the field.

Having no rules isn't all it's cracked up to be!

Fashion police!
If Rex lived in England about 500 years ago, he'd be in big trouble just for wearing purple. King Henry VIII said it was against the law for ordinary people to wear that color.

When I get to the field, everyone is too busy playing to notice my cleats. I don't know if it's the flower power stickers or what, but I play a great game. I even score the winning goal!

"Way to go, Rex!" my team cheers.

After the game, I start thinking about Rosie. I feel bad for yelling at her. As soon as I get home, I'll tell her I'm sorry. And I'll thank her for the good-luck stickers.

23

But Rosie isn't in her room.
She's not watching TV or having a snack.
And she's not in any of her hide-and-seek places.

I have a terrible thought. What if Rosie ran
away because I yelled at her?

She isn't supposed to go anywhere without a
grown-up. But there aren't any rules this weekend,
so maybe she did.

What have I done?

"Mom!" I yell. "Rosie's run away! And it's all my fault!"

"What are you talking about, honey? She's right up there!"

Sure enough, Rosie's up in the tree house—decorating it with stickers. *Whew!* It was just a false alarm. But I'd better make a change before something bad *really* happens.

"Listen up, everyone," I say. "I have a new rule." Mom and Dad look worried.

"Rex's rule is that from now on we all follow the rules!"

Mom and Dad smile. "Deal," they say.

"Deal," says Rosie.

I give her a hug. "I'm sorry I yelled at you."

"That's okay," Rosie says. "But don't do it again!" She sticks a flower sticker on my nose.

We all go out for ice cream after dinner. On the way home, I notice the keep off the grass sign—the one that got me in trouble on Friday. I look at the other signs. What if all those rules weren't there? *Yikes!*

KEEP OFF
THE GRASS

TRASH GOES HERE!

PLEASE DO
NOT PICK THE
FLOWERS

Later that night, Rosie helps me clean up my room. "I guess life without rules can get pretty, uh, sticky," I say as I peel a sticker off my pillow.

"I guess you're right," says Rosie.

"But you know what I found out this weekend?" I say. "I learned that rules are a lot like you."

"What do you mean?" asks Rosie.

"Well, rules can be pretty annoying sometimes," I tell her. "But I'd really miss them if they weren't around!"

Rules rule! Rules and laws keep people safe and help them get along with each other.

I can understand rules and laws!

MAKING CONNECTIONS

There are rules everywhere you go—in your home, in your school, on streets, in parks and stores—everywhere! Sometimes rules can be annoying. But, as Rex finds out, they help keep you safe and keep your community peaceful.

Look Back
- Look at page 6. Why can't Rex ride the roller coaster? Why do you think the park made that rule?
- Look at the picture of Wylie Park on pages 8 and 9. How many rules can you count? Can you think of a reason for each rule?
- What rule does Rosie break on page 18? Why do you think games have so many rules? Why is it important for players to understand the rules?
- On page 27, what is Rex's new rule? Why does he make it?

Try This!
Match the rules with the places you would probably find them.

RULE	PLACE
1. No Diving	A. Zoo
2. Use Crosswalk	B. Library
3. Talk Quietly	C. Park
4. Don't Feed the Animals	D. Pool
5. No Littering	E. Street

Answers: 1.D, 2.E, 3.B, 4.A, 5.C

32